The Prodigal Son

The Prodigal Son

*Insights into Divine Compassion
and Human Behavior*

GEORGES CHEVROT

TRANSLATED BY HELENA SCOTT

Scripture quotations in this work are from the Revised Standard Version, Catholic Edition, copyright 1946, 1952, 1957 by the Division of Christian Education of the National Council of the Churches of Christ in the United States of America, and are used by permission.

Originally published in 1996 by
Association d'Amis et Parents de Msgr. Chevrot, Paris

This edition of *The Prodigal Son* is published, with ecclesiastical approval, by Scepter (U.K.) Ltd, 21 Hinton Avenue, Hounslow TW4 6AP, England. E-mail: general@scepter.demon.co.uk

ISBN 978-0-906138-48-9

Translation copyright © 1999 by Scepter Ltd, London
This edition copyright © 1999 by Scepter Ltd, London
THIRD PRINTING NOVEMBER 2007

ALL RIGHTS RESERVED
No part of this book may be reproduced, stored in a retrieval system, or transmitted in any form or by any means, electronic, mechanical, photocopying, or otherwise, without the prior permission of Scepter (U.K.) Ltd.

PRINTED IN THE UNITED STATES OF AMERICA

Contents

Introduction   9

1 *The Younger Son*   13
    Rejecting love   13
    I will not serve   14
    A branch broken off from the trunk   15
    Sin and freedom   17
    Forgetting God   20

2 *The Elder Son*   23
    The faithful son's sin   23
    The incapacity to love   26

3 *Self-Reflection*   27
    Apostasies of the heart   27
    Our daily sins   28

4 *Realization and Conversion*   32
    Coming to ourselves   34
    New light   34
    Conversion and humility   36
    Do we deserve forgiveness?   37

5 *The Father*   41
    The father's love   41
    God's happiness   44
    The true seriousness of sin   45

6 *A Change of Heart*   47
    A new man   47
    A new conversion every day   49
    We are not converted on our own   51
    On intimate terms with Jesus Christ   53
    The power to make God happy   55

AND HE SAID, "There was a man who had two sons; and the younger of them said to his father, 'Father, give me the share of property that falls to me.' And he divided his living between them. Not many days later, the younger son gathered all he had and took his journey into a far country, and there he squandered his property in loose living. And when he had spent everything, a great famine arose in that country, and he began to be in want. So he went and joined himself to one of the citizens of that country, who sent him into his fields to feed swine. And he would gladly have fed on the pods that the swine ate; and no one gave him anything.

"But when he came to himself he said, 'How many of my father's hired servants have bread enough and to spare, but I perish here with hunger! I will arise and go to my father, and I will say to him, "Father, I have sinned against heaven and before you; I am no longer worthy to be called your son; treat me as one of your hired servants."'

"And he arose and came to his father. But while he was yet at a distance, his father saw him and had compassion, and ran and embraced him and kissed him. And the son said to him, 'Father, I have sinned against heaven and before you; I am no longer worthy to be called your son.'

"But the father said to his servants, 'Bring quickly the best robe, and put it on him; and put a ring on his hand, and shoes on his feet; and bring the fatted calf and kill it, and let us eat and make merry; for this my son was dead and is alive again; he was lost, and is found.' And they began to make merry.

"Now his elder son was in the field; and as he came and drew near to the house, he heard music and dancing. And he called one of the servants and asked what this meant. And he said to him, 'Your brother has come, and your father has killed the fatted calf, because he has received him safe and sound.'

"But he was angry and refused to go in. His father came out and entreated him, but he answered his father, 'Lo, these many years I have served you, and I never disobeyed your command; yet you never gave me a kid, that I might make merry with my friends. But when this son of yours came, who has devoured your living with harlots, you killed for him the fatted calf!'

"And he said to him, 'Son, you are always with me, and all that is mine is yours. It was fitting to make merry and be glad, for this your brother was dead and is alive; he was lost and is found.'"

— Luke 15: 11–32

Introduction

The parable of the Good Shepherd has been called a little gospel within the Gospel. That's going a bit far; it does not, after all, contain all the riches of Christian doctrine. However, in this parable our Lord is making a moving appeal to us to be converted.

Repent. Be converted. Begin again. These are the three stages of the spiritual life.

Today, to stimulate our repentance, let's look at what the parable teaches us about the evil of sin and the wretched state of the sinner.

We have to admit: if this parable did not contain a hidden meaning that we had to try to find, it would be a most unlikely sounding story.

A man had two sons. Which of the two would you wish to be like? One was unable to look after his soul; the other was unable to give his heart. Both saddened their father, both treated him harshly, both failed to recognize how good he was to them—one through disobeying and the other in spite of obeying.

Which of them would you want to be like? The spendthrift or the calculating one? Because there is no third son we can claim a likeness to, we are forced to agree that we are one or the other . . . or perhaps both the one and the other.

They are very strange sons indeed. But we also have to add that they have a very strange father, one who doesn't give a thought to his own dignity and who doesn't exercise his authority. Why? He does nothing to stand in the way of his younger son's insolence, stupidity, and whims. Not only does he not cut off his allowance, which any of you would have done in his place, but he doesn't even try to reason with him. Just listen to the younger brother: *"Father, give me the share of the property that falls to me." And he divided his living between them.* As simple as that. He lets himself be plundered by the boy without so much as a murmur of protest.

And the end of the story is no more edifying than the beginning. When his older son refuses to come and share the feast, lo and behold, it is the father who goes out to beg him to come in. What sort of house is this, where the children give the orders? When will this father ever say, just for once, "I want you to do this," "I command you to . . ."? This father has brought up his children very badly indeed, as I'm sure you will agree.

But we aren't in any house here on earth. This father who asks instead of ordering, who gives in and cannot say No, who forgives instead of punishing . . . this father has no equal here on earth. It is our Father in Heaven, and St. John has told us his name: "God is love."

We recognize him by the traits shown in the parable: this God who keeps silent and stays in the background, this God who gives and forgives. He has given us just one law: "Thou shalt love." In the Father's house the children do not work for a salary; they are happy to share their father's labors, and their father is happy to share his wealth with them. Their one ambition is to love each other more and more, forever.

This household, which has no equivalent among families here on earth, nevertheless does exist on earth. We belong to it: it is the Church, which, by incorporat-

Introduction

ing us into Jesus Christ, has made us God's children. In the Church and through it, we share everything with our brothers and sisters and share everything with our Father in Heaven.

This happy state, begun in us by Baptism, strengthened by Confirmation, increased by the Eucharist, is what we call the state of grace.

Love is the only law in the Father's house.

But love has one condition: freedom. No living being can be forced to love, as no one can be loved by force. Freedom is the condition for love, and love is the endless renewing of freedom. God, who loves us—because he loves us and because he expects love from us and wants nothing but love—has run the great risk of love, and the great risk of giving us freedom.

We are able—alas, we have the power, amazing and woeful as it is—to refuse him or haggle with him over our love. That is the story of the two sons in the parable, the story of sin, our own story.

Let's talk first about grave sin: the sin that makes us lose the state of grace, that destroys God's life in us.

1. *The Younger Son*

Rejecting love

The younger of them said to his father, "Father, give me the share of property that falls to me." And he divided his living between them. Not many days later, the younger son gathered all he had and took his journey into a far country.

No, the father could not hold him back by force. The doors of his house are not bolted. Love is infinitely demanding, but it cannot be demanded. Sin, the refusal of love, shows straightaway that it is a disorder. The son gives the orders, the father obeys: the world is turned topsy-turvy.

We have all left our Father's house in the person of Adam, the first sinner. Each of our sins has its roots in that first departure. Each of our sins is a repetition of original sin. What did Adam, the first sinner, want? Created free by a privilege that was unique in the whole of creation, he wanted to use his freedom as *he* chose. Not to obey but to command.

You remember how the story is told in the Bible? The forbidden fruit is the fruit of the tree of the knowledge of good and evil. If they eat it, the tempter whispers to them, they will be like God, because they themselves will be able to decide what is good and what is evil. It will no longer be God who determines good and evil but themselves. They will be their own masters. Adam wanted to be his own master; he chose the freedom of being himself, independent of God, without God, and therefore far from God . . . and he *took his journey into a far country*.

The younger son in the parable, and like him anyone who voluntarily commits a grave sin (I remind you that this is the only kind we are considering at the moment: grave sin, which many of you have never committed), this sinner renewed that separation, Adam's departure from God. He traveled away. He left his father. That is what sin consists of.

I will not serve

Don't be led astray by the details of the parable. As the older son will refer to his brother's debaucheries, we might conclude that that was what the younger son's sin consisted of, and reduce the lesson of the parable to his offenses against morality. Many Catholics think of sin as breaking the sixth commandment only. They haven't sinned against that commandment, so they haven't sinned.

In their defense, it is true that many preachers, when they speak about sin, seem, by the description they give of it, to be looking only at those particular vices. But because this kind of sin is obviously widespread, don't let's conclude that it is the most serious sin.

Impiety, which the prophets of Israel compared to adultery; anger, and all forms of homicide; greed, avarice, and all forms of theft; spite, calumny, and all forms of lying; without forgetting faults of omission, as, for example, the sin of the rich man who walks heedlessly past Lazarus as he lies at his door . . . all these kinds of sin are no less serious than sins of impurity. And sin, properly so called, does not reside in these categories of faults.

The younger son leaves his father not because he wishes to lead a dissolute life but because he no longer wants to obey his father. He wants to take his father's place.

David, holy King David, as he is called, who is so frequently proposed to us as a model for penitents in the Bible and in the liturgy, was guilty of adultery, murder, and scandal. But when he looks at himself, when he examines his sin before God, he does not think of the scandal he has caused, or the death he has brought about, or the adultery he has committed: *Tibi soli peccavi,* against thee, thee alone, have I sinned.

The prodigal son's sin began the day he stopped loving his father above everything, more than himself. His sin grew progressively as he began to feel stifled in that house, whose monotony weighed heavily on him. As his love fell back on himself, selfishness gained the upper hand over the love he had had for his father up till then. His sin started in his mind. It is always there that we need to detect sin. It started when he said to himself, "I have a perfect right to act as I choose. After all, I am answerable only to myself." Sin is the revolt of the "self" against God: it is the *non serviam,* I will not serve, of the bad angels.

A branch broken off from the trunk

But the father of the prodigal son could do nothing except let him go. If he did not hold back his ungrateful son, perhaps you are wondering why, in any case, he gave him the whole of his inheritance. Why? Because our Father in Heaven makes his sun rise and his rain fall on the field of the wicked and impious as well as on the field of the good and just. Much good it would do our Father in Heaven to deprive the sinner of his possessions, if he has lost his son's love. His only concern is for our love. The sinner wants to have nothing more to do with him; the only thing he values is his father's money . . . so let him have it, let him keep it, take it away, and get drunk on it. . . .

And this young man, who wants his independence, can only get it by using what his father gives him.

He squandered his property. The sinner offends God with what he has received from God. To achieve his goal the sinner uses his intelligence, which God gave him when he created him in his own image and likeness. The sinner corners for himself the good things on earth that God had given to the community of mankind. The money he amasses will be the means to slake his passions and guard his own interests. He makes use of God's gifts to defy God.

Dissipavit substantiam—he squandered his property. These words have a deeper level of meaning when the sinner is a Christian. For it would be untrue to say that all the deeds of a sinner are bad. The outward behavior of many sinners is irreproachable. Many of them do good. Their deeds are not all bad, but they are wasted. They are lost for Heaven because supernatural merit belongs to the state of grace. This substance, this property that the sinful Christian squanders, is his share in the inheritance of Heaven. It is eternal life, which he had from God and which is something of God himself. A sinful Christian is merely a branch broken off from the trunk. He receives no more sap; he is deprived of life, he withers and will soon be a stick of dead wood fit only for the fire. Nothing is left to him of the reserves he had stored up through his prayers, efforts, faith, and zeal. He has ruined himself.

Dissipavit substantiam vivendo luxuriose—he squandered his property in loose living. Again, let's not translate this in a way that would suggest the prodigal son's whole case was merely a question of self-indulgence. *Luxuriose* would be better rendered as "without restraint," like someone who has lost all self-control. And this perfectly characterizes the wretched state of someone who refuses God's love. He wants to be his own master, his only master, and straightaway he loses mastery over himself. He was aiming to gain his freedom, but in reality he has cast it away.

Sin and freedom

Let's not believe that sin is the illegitimate use of freedom. Sin kills freedom, because freedom is fundamentally and essentially linked to love, as we have seen. Let's not reason as philosophers but as Christians. Freedom is not the choice between good and evil; freedom disappears as soon as we choose evil. For example, before telling a lie I am free; if I tell the truth, I am still free; if I tell a lie, I am chained to my lie.

And the same is true of all other sins.

When he left his father's house, the younger son did not carry his freedom with him. He carried its corpse. He was to experience this only too bitterly, first in the nausea following on his debauchery, and then in the terrible pangs of his hunger. His freedom was dead. He who had been so proud of having gained his freedom would be reduced to hiring himself out to a pagan. And he, a Jew, would have to look after unclean animals. Every morning he would have to muck out the pigsty. Jesus will spell it out quite clearly, using the solemn formula: "Truly I say to you, whoever commits sin is a slave to sin."

The expression "to give oneself up to sin" holds a great deal of truth. The word virtue comes from *virtus*, courage, strength, virility; and virtue can be achieved only at the cost of a great effort. By contrast, one gives oneself up to evil, one lets oneself go. The sinner follows the downward slope of his passions; all he has to do is just let himself slide.

Freedom to do evil is no more than a caricature of freedom. Man is necessarily tied to the object of his love. If he loves God and his brothers and sisters, these ties ennoble him and exalt his freedom; if he obeys only his self-love, he is bound by ties that degrade him and make his freedom sterile. Man experiences either the attachment of a worker to a task that enhances his own value or the attachment of a miser to the gold that enslaves him; either the disinterested love of the common good, which makes man great, or the scheming love of the ambitious man who is himself a captive in the hands of people who manipulate his interests; either the attachment of a husband to the affections of his home, which support and strengthen him, or the attachment of an unfaithful spouse to a woman who demands total possession of his heart, his time, his money, and, probably, his good name. *Servus est peccati,* he is the slave of sin.

And the law of momentum applies in morals as it does in physics: the longer an object's fall lasts, the faster and the deeper the object goes. In vain does the sinner set himself limits he is not to overstep. Whatever passion he gives in to, the moment it is satisfied it demands newer and stronger satisfactions. Notice how in virtue we never rise as high as we were expecting to, while, in sinning, we always go lower than we had foreseen. We always fall short of the good we would like to carry out, and we always go beyond the evil we believe we can allow ourselves. There are limits to our capacity for holiness. There are none to our capacity for sin. The sinner has turned his back on his own freedom.

Sin, which perverts the heart, does not change its nature. Man's heart is still infinite in its desires. Created to love God above all things, man may change the object of his passion but not his way of loving. He *will* love infinitely, he *will* adore; and if the object of his love is no longer God, then alas, it is an idol. Having turned away from God, he transfers his great desires to the passion to which he is chained, which has enslaved him, and eventually reaches the point where he sins out of habit, without enjoyment, because it is the day, because it is time, because it is the occasion. He is bound to the service of a master who does not pay.

It is this state of slavery that our Blessed Lord, in this parable, wanted to highlight, by picturing a famine breaking out in the country where the young prodigal was living. There is no more water in the streams, the grass is scorched, the harvests are ruined, the trees bear no more fruit, and bread is so rare that its price soars. *And he began to be in want. So he went and joined himself to one of the citizens of that country, who sent him into his fields to feed swine. And he would gladly have fed on the pods that the swine ate; and no one gave him anything.*

Critics, who are incapable of respecting a masterpiece, allege that these details are forced and unlifelike. What farmworker, they say, in such a case, would not have taken a handful of the husks out of the pigs' ration, to eat himself? No doubt about it at all. But that is to bypass the storyteller's intention. Jesus wants to bring home to us the horrible loneliness of the sinner. He has fallen lower than the animals he watches over. The farm owner is concerned about feeding his pigs, but no one at all is concerned about him. It doesn't occur to anyone to give him something to eat. The pig-farmer values the fat on his animals more highly than his servant's life. The prodigal is abandoned by everyone.

Forgetting God

With all this, however, we still have not underlined the chief factor that characterizes the sinner's unhappy state: his ruin, his poverty, his servitude . . . are all the result of leaving his father's house. To enjoy his freedom the younger son went away to a far country. And St. Augustine gives us the key to these two words: *regio longinqua, quae est oblivio Dei,* a far country, which is the forgetting of God.

He is in the country of forgetting. Sordid and wretched, the man who was once so rich and has become a swineherd now lacks all that makes up a man's life: bread, home, friendship, love, dignity, self-respect, and above all, hope; because his wretched state will never end. Forever is his freedom lost, forever has he lost everything, even his memory, and that is the crux of the drama. We know from the rest of the story that he will recover his memory: *when he comes to himself.* But at this point he is a stranger to himself. He has forgotten all his past life, he has forgotten his father—*oblivio Dei.* He had completely failed to recognize his father's love, the day when he refused to give him his own! Was he really going to spend much time thinking about his father's house, which he had found so oppressive? He had to forget it so as to burn his boats. He had to get as far away as possible so that no one would come looking for him. In order to live outside anyone's control and so be independent, he had to forget what he had left behind. And he traveled to a distant country where he could begin his life anew, in a foreign land where nobody knew him, in a pagan country where there would be no synagogue to go to. He had to forget, to cast out the memory of his father, so as to stifle his last scruples . . . or the first stirrings of remorse.

    The psalmist of old knew all about this: "The wicked man has said in his heart, there is no God." God can't be expelled from the universe. Of course not. But the sinner doesn't want there to be a God to bother him. So he goes away and behaves as though God didn't exist! This exclusion of God is not always explicit. To start with, at least, some sinners take refuge behind a possible excuse: I was looking for pleasure; I wanted to satisfy my ambition, to take revenge . . . but I never intended to offend God! I never even thought of him. . . . And look what they have just said: they never even thought of him—*oblivio Dei:* God was forgotten. All things considered, what sort of excuse is that? Wouldn't it be truer to say: God was rejected in their forgetting him?

Were you praying, brother, when you were meditating on your revenge? When you were planning a shady trick in order to get ahead? Could you still say, at that moment, "Thy will be done"? Then face it: you were playing hide-and-seek with God. You were running away from him and had no wish to pray.

And the sinner who does still pray? The sinner who still prays is risking shipwreck, but he has not sunk completely; a life belt may yet bring him to the shore. The sinner who has totally forsaken his freedom, who has passed from freedom to slavery... he doesn't pray any more. And that is how one can be sure of recognizing a sinner: he cannot pray. God is absent from his mind and his life. God no longer exists for him. It is the last stage in the rejection of love.

Hopeless, starving, in the stink of a pigsty, the son who has refused his father's love no longer remembers him. But his father has not forgotten his son. Who will restore his lost memory to the outcast? We will see the answer later on; but first we will go back to his father's house without him to meet the other sinner, who continues to live at his father's side—but without giving him all his love.

2. *The Elder Son*

The faithful son's sin

After the sin of the rebel, the apostate, the unfaithful son, the sin that has just filled us with horror, we must now talk about the sin of the faithful son, the son who practices his faith but whose soul lacks depth. His is the camouflaged, discreet sin, unsuspected sometimes even by the person who commits it: the sin of most of us. For this son, the elder one, was outwardly a model of obedience. *Lo, these many years I have served you, and I never disobeyed your command.* . . . And his father doesn't contradict him at all.

This son has never disobeyed, unlike the younger one. He could be held up as an example. And the neighbors undoubtedly thought so, as they did their best to console the father for his disgrace: "Don't keep thinking about the son who has gone, friend; your elder son at least is still with you. His faithfulness should lessen your suffering." And we would have had nothing but praise for him, were it not for this unexpected incident that laid bare his heart.

Yes, most people think they are better than the rest. And we ourselves are quite happy to think that any talk of sinners applies to others, not to us. And then something happens unexpectedly, taking us by surprise and making us recognize that we do indeed belong to the family of sinners.

All the saints knew this. St. Francis of Assisi was sincere; he was not exaggerating, and still less indulging in false humility, when he declared himself before God "the greatest of sinners: Francis of Assisi." And Paul wrote to Timothy with equal sincerity, "Christ Jesus came into the world to save sinners—of whom I am the foremost!" St. Paul called himself the last among the apostles and the first among sinners.

But when people are blindly convinced of their own merits, providence, as we ourselves have perhaps experienced, takes care to undeceive them by some unexpected event, as happened to the elder son.

Beneath his virtuous exterior he allows us a sudden glimpse of the evil sentiments hidden in the depths of his heart, which he has been suppressing, perhaps, but which will explode in a flash, at the touch of his anger. In a moment this model of obedience stands revealed in all his jealousy, envy, avarice, malice, and hard-heartedness: *Lo, these many years I have served you.*

This last bit really hurts us. When had his father ever considered him as a slave or even a servant? "I do not call you servants any longer," says Jesus to the Twelve, "I have called you my friends."

His father underlines the inappropriateness of the elder son's language: *Son, you are always with me.* "I have always treated you as a son. . . . My joy was to have you near me . . . while you were keeping a tally of the services you were rendering me . . . !"

Lo, these many years I have served you! Behind the reproach lies an unspoken but ill-concealed regret: "If it were all to do again, I wouldn't be so naïve! I'd take things easy, like the younger son. Piety and obedience have brought me no gain, but I've never

The Elder Son

shirked any task. I've been out in all kinds of weather. I've worked double since that depraved boy left, so that the farm shouldn't suffer by his absence. And you've never had the slightest consideration for me. You've never given me so much as a young goat to share with my friends."

"Have I ever refused you one?" must have been his father's thought. "If you had wanted one, you had only to take it. I wouldn't have grudged it! *All that is mine is yours.* How could I have imagined that if you wanted something you wouldn't tell me? How could I have supposed you would be too afraid of me to ask? Is that all the confidence you had in my kindness toward you?"

And the son tried to find whatever would wound his father's heart most cruelly. No, "tried to find" is not right, because when you are angry you come straight out with the words that will hurt most and that you can never unsay!

When this son of yours came . . .—oh, he takes good care not to say "my brother"; he has nothing in common with that crook. . . . "But when this son of yours came back, who has eaten up your property with prostitutes, because it was with your savings that he launched out on his orgies, wasn't it! With your property, patiently amassed by your labor—by our labor. If virtue is not rewarded, you certainly can't say the same of vice. . . . Oh, how stupid I was not to do the same as he did! Because that fine gentleman comes back starving, you have killed the fatted calf for him—a magnificent animal we were to have sold in the market next week, which would have brought us in a tidy sum!"

The incapacity to love

We can learn a lot from seeing the exact circumstances in which this son, who has always been so obedient, finally refuses his father's love. His stumbling block is a truth St. John the Apostle stated, one that we sometimes find hard to admit: "Those who say, 'I love God,' and hate their brothers or sisters, are liars." This has often seemed somewhat excessive to us. God and our neighbor constitute two separate domains. God is lovable above all things, and I owe him adoration and obedience. Why bring between God and myself people who are certainly not worthy of being loved? God, yes, always; my neighbor—well, that depends.... No, our Lord told us. No, St. John repeats. You can't say that you love your father if you don't love your brother.

Here, then, is the screen that hides God from us, preventing us from coming close to him or turning us farther away from him: our terrible selfishness, our unbearable self-love. It's the self that we fall back on endlessly, the selfishness that drove the younger son to leave his father's house, the selfishness that prevented the elder son from welcoming his brother home.

All of us are selfish. All sinners. We would have every reason to despair, were it not that our Lord came to call sinners, not the just.

How he goes about making us into loving children we will see later. For the moment, let us become aware of our own poverty-stricken state.

3. Self-Reflection

Apostasies of the heart

In commenting on these texts from the Gospel I have avoided as much as possible applying them too specifically, and I have done that on purpose. The second part of all meditation—reflecting on oneself, which is the most important part—is something we must each do for ourselves, and it is best done alone. Its usefulness does not consist in reckoning up the number of your sins—I beg you not to do that. God has already forgiven you for them, and you would be insulting his mercy if you doubted his forgiveness. No, what you need to do is recognize your—our—sinful condition, which will keep us really humble and, most of all, will invite us to thank God for the love he has for us in spite of our unworthiness. Understanding that we are sinners is itself a great grace, because we can be saved only if we fully recognize that we are lost.

In this consideration of our sinfulness, we will take into account this or that particularly grave fault which perhaps made us lose the state of grace, happily recovered afterward. But I draw your attention to this point: we distinguish between mortal sin and venial sin, and quite rightly, since in theory it is a very useful distinction. But let us not abuse this distinction in practice;

because, first, it is often very difficult to know whether the three conditions that constitute mortal sin were present: grave matter, full knowledge, and full consent. What's more, this difficulty is often the cause of distressing scruples for some. How right St. Joan of Arc was, against the learned men who asked her if she believed she was in a state of grace: "If I am, may God keep me in it. If I am not, may God restore me to it."

But this habit of distinguishing between mortal sin and venial sin can also produce a tendency to laxity in us: "As long as it's not a mortal sin. . . ." Oh, yes? And look at all the abuses that leads to! It was a very holy nun who called deliberate venial sin "the apostasy of the heart."

Our daily sins

For Christians, there is another distinction to make, between material sin and formal sin. On the one hand, there are the sins that take us by surprise—sins committed out of weakness, which St. Augustine called *peccata quotidiana,* our daily sins. As there is daily bread, so there are daily sins. The author of *The Imitation of Christ* echoes St. Augustine: "For as long as we are in this weak body, we cannot be without sin." Of course, we cannot avoid experiencing the pressure of sin but that does not imply that we always consent deliberately. And St. Augustine declared that those sins which take us by surprise, because of our weakness, the sins we commit every day—he said this in an instruction given to catechumens whom he was preparing to make their First Communion—all those sins are forgiven by the words we say in the Lord's Prayer: *dimitte nobis debita nostra,* forgive us our trespasses; and they are all forgiven.

And, on the other hand, there are the sins and faults we freely consent to and *a fortiori* are deliberate faults: a definite duty, something that is clearly God's will and that we deliberately omit, put off till later, or refuse. In that case there is formal sin, as opposed to purely material sin. And this sin resides precisely in the haggling over love and the refusal to love, which are the subject of our meditation. Now, an enlightened Christian, who wishes to stay faithful, does not need a theologian's declaration that these are mortal sins before reproaching himself or herself for them and trying not to commit them.

It not infrequently happens that this positive refusal of love is over a slight fault rather than faults that are held to be serious. Yes, but that is precisely what we want to try and measure: our selfishness in the face of God's love.

It may be helpful for some—not for the scrupulous—to reread chapter 23 of St. Matthew's Gospel, transposing to our epoch and our way of life the reproaches pronounced by our Lord against the Pharisees of his time: "You strain out a gnat and swallow a camel." Let's take care not to be the sort of Catholics who accuse themselves of distractions in prayer or not having gone to Mass when they were ill in bed—how could they have gone?—and who don't mention some murderous little bit of calumny. They accuse themselves of having omitted religious practices—the tithe of mint and fennel and cumin—while they do not worry about omitting the weightier matters of the law.... Jesus lists them: justice and mercy and faith. It is these, says Jesus, we ought to practice, without neglecting the others.

St. John wrote to the angel of the Church at Ephesus, with a message from the Lord: "I know your works, your toil and your patient endurance. I know that you cannot tolerate evildoers;... that you are enduring patiently and bearing up for the sake of my name, and that you have not grown weary. But I have this against you, that you have abandoned the love you had at first." And perhaps you recognize yourself in this account. Because you sincerely hate evil, and you love our Lord, many of you have suffered for him.... Look carefully and see, nevertheless, whether you haven't slackened off a little from your former love, since last year... a slackening-off in your vigilance against your defects, in your efforts toward virtue; a little weakening in your faith, in your charity; carelessness in prayer....

Whatever the result of your examination of conscience—although it ought to give rise to regret and humility—it shouldn't cast you into a state of discouragement. It is not God who discourages us. All temptations to discouragement deserve the name temptation and originate from the devil. When we are seeking to love God as much as we can, discouragement never comes from him, ever.

I also invite you to say, and to say again, the prayer we find in chapter 9 of the fourth book of the *Imitation*. It is a magnificent prayer of offering that we can also often say before receiving Holy Communion and as preparation for it. I will leave it to you to read the whole prayer and will just give you the second paragraph here: "Lord, I bring you all my sins." A strange offering at first sight, but one that God will not refuse, not only because we are sorry for them but because all the sins that have been forgiven us are soaked in his Son's blood. "Lord, I bring you all my sins and all the wrong things I have done in your sight and in the sight of your holy angels, from the very first day I was capable of sinning, right up to this present time. I offer them on your altar of atonement so that you may burn them all together, consume them in the flame of your love, wipe out all the stains of my sins and cleanse my conscience from every wrong. Renew in me the gift of your grace which I lost by sinning; grant me in abundance all I need, and in your mercy receive me and give me the kiss of peace."

4. Realization and Conversion

Blessed is he whose transgression is forgiven, whose sin is covered. Blessed is the man to whom the Lord imputes no iniquity, and in whose spirit there is no deceit. When I declared not my sin, my body wasted away through my groaning all day long. For day and night thy hand was heavy upon me; my strength was dried up as by the heat of summer. I acknowledged my sin to thee, and I did not hide my iniquity; I said, "I will confess my transgressions to the Lord"; then thou didst forgive the guilt of my sin.

— Psalm 32(31): 1–5

That which was from the beginning, which we have heard, which we have seen with our eyes, which we have looked upon and touched with our hands, concerning the word of life—the life was made manifest and we saw it and testify to it and proclaim to you the eternal life which was with the Father and was made manifest to us—that which we have seen and heard we proclaim also to you, so that you may have fellowship with us; and our fellowship is with the Father and with his Son Jesus Christ. And we are writing this that our joy may be complete. This is the message we have heard from him and proclaim to you, that God is light and in him is no darkness at all. If we say we have fellowship with him while we walk in darkness, we lie and do not live according to the truth; but if we walk in the light as he is in the light we have fellowship with one another, and the blood of Jesus his Son cleanses us from all sin. If we say we have no sin, we deceive ourselves, and the

Realization and Conversion

truth is not in us. If we confess our sins, he is faithful and just, and will forgive our sins and cleanse us from all unrighteousness. If we say we have not sinned, we make him a liar, and his word is not in us. My little children, I am writing this to you so that you may not sin; but if any one does sin, we have an advocate with the Father, Jesus Christ the righteous; and he is the expiation for our sins, and not for ours only but also for the sins of the whole world.

— 1 John 1: 1–2: 2

After this he went out, and saw a tax collector, named Levi, sitting at the tax office; and he said to him, "Follow me." And he left everything and rose and followed him. And Levi made him a great feast in his house; and there was a large company of tax collectors and others sitting at table with them. And the Pharisees and their scribes murmured against his disciples, saying, "Why do you eat and drink with tax collectors and sinners?" And Jesus answered them, "Those who are well have no need of a physician, but those who are sick; I have not come to call the righteous, but sinners to repentance." And they said to him, "The disciples of John fast often and offer prayers, and so do the disciples of the Pharisees, but yours eat and drink."

— Luke 5: 27–33

The story of the prodigal son has allowed us to fathom the depths of the sinner's wretched state; and the story of the calculating son has shown us that we all belong to the race of sinners and that it takes very little for us to discover the root of all sins within ourselves. We have also said our *mea culpa*, without either being presumptuous or getting discouraged. Our Lord is calling every one of us to be converted: now let us look and see what this conversion actually consists of.

Coming to ourselves

When he came to himself . . . We left the prodigal son in the depths of degradation, humbled, shamed, and starving. . . . From the beginning of his sad escapade he had not been master of his own soul. He did not know himself as he really was. "The man who loves himself alone," writes Pascal, "hates nothing so much as to be alone with himself." But because God wants to save us, the time comes, sooner or later, when the sinner comes to himself, brought by God's mercy.

The unmindful son wouldn't have come to himself had not a special grace from the Holy Spirit made him turn inward on himself, reminding him of everything he had forgotten: *regio longinqua, oblivio Dei.* He had forgotten God, but God did not forget him.

But how to break down the doors of that memory which remained obstinately closed and, so far, impermeable to grace? To do that, God has all the means he wants. He quite often uses physical or moral trials. And under the blows of failures, disappointments, and suffering, the sinner comes to himself—where the grace of God has been waiting for him.

New light

But when he came to himself he said, "How many of my father's hired servants have bread enough and to spare, but I perish here with hunger!" There can be no doubt that when the prodigal came to himself, the first and almost the only thing he was conscious of was his own wretched state. He did not yet see the malice of his sin. It is too

Realization and Conversion

early for that; he will see it later. He sees only his own destitution and suffering, which are apparently hopeless: *I perish here with hunger.*

Get hold of this fact: we don't understand the seriousness of sin until after we have been converted and, often, not till several years after. I say this to calm the worry of some Christians who have turned away from sin and, once they comprehend the seriousness of their faults, are afraid that they did not confess those former sins properly. They now see them as being so much more serious. It is a new light that God is sending you; when you committed those sins you did not possess the light that God has given you today. It is a new grace that God is sending you. So don't worry about it. It is only after we have been converted that we really understand the seriousness of our sin: we didn't understand it before. We need to be back on our feet and to have climbed out of the pit before we can really tell how deep it was.

I perish here with hunger. The prodigal could have carried on chewing over his own misery endlessly; he would never have got out of it if God's grace had not come to his aid. And what does God do when he enlightens a sinner's conscience? Because God has all sorts of means at his disposal, he generally reminds them of their own history: all that they had, all they have abandoned, all they have lost. Spurred on by his hunger, the prodigal reviews the years of his youth. He recalls his father's house: the house where one had to love and therefore to obey, but where one never lacked for anything. In his mind's eye he again saw his father's house, such a welcoming house, where travelers were invited in to sit down and eat, and where the least of the hired hands had bread and to spare.

It still exists, the house from which he has run so very far away. His father still exists. But *he* can no longer call himself his son. He has made himself unworthy to bear his father's name. But his father has not changed. His father has stayed the same: the man who loved him too much to force him to stay at home; his father, whose heart he has broken, whose property he has squandered, whom he has afflicted, dishonored... his father!

The prodigal is ruined. He has lost everything, absolutely everything. Not a single hand will be held out to him; everyone will turn pitilessly away from him; he deserves no better, after what he has done. He has nothing left in the world, nothing... except his father.

Oh, if only his father could see the misfortune to which he has fallen! His poor father... he has given his father such a poor return for all his affection. It is the first time he has ever recognized the terrible suffering his departure has caused his father. His father! How he must have suffered! How he must still be suffering! More even than himself, amidst his pigs. And with the thought, his own suffering becomes less acute to him than his father's. He is on his way to repentance. He wakes up to his own wickedness, and the first tears of remorse run down his hollow cheeks at the thought of his father.

Conversion and humility

But remember that remorse is not yet conversion. If I searched the world over, he thinks, I would never find a house like my father's, which I left so wickedly. If any

Realization and Conversion

house can still receive the outcast I have become, it is that one. My father can do whatever he likes to me. He can treat me like a slave, since I am no longer worthy to be called his son. I would rather be the last person in his house than live anywhere else for a day longer. "I will set off, I will go back to him, I will not try to make any excuses for my behavior, because it is inexcusable. I will confess my guilt before him: Father, I have offended you, and by offending you I have sinned against Heaven; treat me with the utmost harshness, I have deserved it. I will accept it all, as long as I am no longer far from you, as long as I am no longer plunged in wretchedness."

And he arose and came to his father.

Do we deserve forgiveness?

Hold on! say some champions of morality. A very comfortable conversion! And a very suspect kind of repentance! Can't you see that the boy hasn't really changed? He is still totally selfish. He is going back home to get bread to eat, and he is calculating on his father's goodness. He scorned his father's house when he left it. If he is going back—he says so himself—it is only because the servants there have plenty to eat. Let him start off by changing his lazy life! He is young, he can work, he has had a good education . . . he should go somewhere where he can find some job. Every fault demands expiation! He should really reform his ways, lead a tough life perhaps, subject himself to harsh punishment if he wants to show that his repentance is sincere. And when he has proved that he has really renounced his evil ways, then he should write to his father, humbly begging his forgiveness, asking for a tiny place in the home he deserted.

This comes down to saying that he should wait till he *deserves* to be forgiven and that he should first prove that his repentance is sincere. But . . . how much time will you give him for his rehabilitation? How long will it take before he is worthy to cross his father's threshold? Will he ever be worthy? And for the whole of that time, his father will just have to wait, won't he? His poor father, inconsolable from the moment he left . . .

You are not the kind of people to use such severe language. In fact, I suspect you would look for arguments in favor of the sinner's repentance, the decision he made when once he was nauseated by his sin. You will point out to me the humility of his repentance: that he is going back to humble himself before his father; he recognizes that he is no longer worthy to be treated as a son. Far from refusing to expiate his misbehavior, he is voluntarily going to face whatever punishment his father may wish to impose on him. He will work as a hired servant, as a slave, without spending anything on himself, so as to be able, if possible, to buy back the fields that had to be sold when he barefacedly claimed his part of the inheritance. He has no doubt that his life will be a hard one from now on. When one has tasted the forbidden fruit, obedience henceforth becomes very hard. He can imagine the humiliations awaiting him when the neighbors, the servants, and his elder brother see him coming back in his rags, in his destitution, because he's got nothing left . . . he has sold his ring, the last outward sign of being a free man, long since.

Won't they all jeer at him?

And these thoughts, and plenty of others no less depressing, assail the young man's mind as he hobbles painfully on bare feet, soon cut and bleeding, toward his father's house.

You who are so compassionate, I can see you are very ready to defend the guilty son. Isn't the homeward road itself, you will say, on which he is enduring so much pain, already the beginning of his expiation?

And, nevertheless, people who lean toward pity mistake the lesson of the parable just as much as those who are inclined to be severe. Both alike want the sinner to merit his forgiveness.

It is as moralists that we talk about repentance and pass judgement on it. "Lord, I did sin, but I have been converted. I renounce my past; I have sacrificed my sinful passions to you; I have done a long penance; I have undertaken plenty of fasts and given alms in abundance. . . . Now, Lord, will you not receive me into your house once again?"

Can't you see that it is precisely in that sort of attitude that calculating selfishness really lies? Are we going to give pride a place in our repentance? We shouldn't modify the facts of the parable by making the condition for the prodigal's return other than one of total humiliation. The young man has no grounds on which to plead his cause before his father. He has not made any sacrifice; all he renounced were the pods the pigs ate—some renunciation! He goes home because he is starving, because he can't take any more, because he is at the end of his tether. He doesn't try to pass himself off as a model of penance; he goes home because he has plumbed the depths of wretchedness and his only chance of getting out is to go and knock on his father's door.

It is perfectly true that he stayed away from his father as long as he possibly could. And he goes home because he can't take any more, because it is his very last hope; he knows quite well that he is utterly contemptible and that people have the right to turn their heads away as he goes by. He knows this; he shouts it aloud. But he also knows that there is one person in the whole world who is capable of not rejecting him: his father, to whom he has nothing to give. Yes, his father, whom he has offended so badly, is the only person who will consent to take him back.

And he arose and came to his father.

5. The Father

The father's love

Don't let's imagine that we know better than our Lord; let's not make ourselves look foolish by trying to correct his parable. Let's read it just as he told it. You have noticed how the divine narrator wasted no time on analyzing the sinner's feelings. We suddenly find ourselves back at his father's house, without any stages in between. And what we need to understand is that this is where the point of the parable lies, in the sudden, unexpected conversion; and that the main character in the parable is the father. It is not the prodigal spendthrift son, any more than it is the recalcitrant elder son. The main character is the father.

The whole parable is played out around the father: the father flouted by his younger son; the father misunderstood by the elder; the father who opens his doors to the disobedient son; the father who humbly begs the obedient one to come in. The two sons are there to make the figure of the father stand out. And St. Luke took good care to tell us when it was that our Lord told this parable: it was to reply to the scribes and the Pharisees, who were indignant to see him welcoming publicans and sinners. We need to recognize how God receives the sinners who come to him—who come to him without merit; who come to him empty-handed and dirty—and how his mercy forgives our wretchedness. Now we are at the center of the parable.

THE PRODIGAL SON

In the distance, the prodigal son can now make out his father's farm and the surrounding lands. He is afraid; he slackens his pace, and his heart starts beating faster. One anguished thought lies heavy on his heart: what if they turn him away? Basically that would be only what he deserves. Only now does he begin to glimpse the evil of his sin. Now he can feel in his very flesh how unbelievably harshly he treated his father. Will he be able to look him in the face? Too bad if he incurs his father's just anger. He must at least confess his offense, unforgivable as it is. Night will soon fall. He goes forward slowly. His legs will hardly carry him.

But there is another heart, which is beating still faster than his own: the heart of his father, who has never for an instant ceased to grieve for his younger son's absence. Every evening since that fatal day he has come and stood at the end of the terrace, where he gets a good view over all the surrounding countryside. Every evening he has scrutinized the roads around, and every evening he has gone back inside with his heart a little heavier than before. And the following day he has gone up to the terrace again. . . . You never know. Supposing his son were to come back? But no. What a foolish hope! His child is lost, his child is dead.

Months and years have gone by . . . and his son has not yet returned. And still his hope outweighs his despair. His hope is stronger than anything else. Every evening he comes back to wait for his son's return.

What would have happened if that evening, tired of waiting in vain, he had not gone? If, as the prodigal came to his father's land, he had met only a servant, who, taking him for a vagabond, had thrown him off the estate without more ado? . . . And one shudders to

The Father

think of what would have happened if he had met his brother; if . . . All sorts of things could have happened and any one of them might have deprived the sinner of his forgiveness forever.

Plenty of you could bear witness to the fact that it would have taken very little to prevent you from relieving your consciences one evening of a sin that was weighing you down. The church might have been closed, or the priest you were looking for might have been away. . . . Would you have gone back the next day? How did it come about that you were in fact able to receive the forgiveness you needed exactly when you were ready for it? Just by chance? Don't you believe it. Someone arranged it all, the someone who was waiting for you: our Father.

The father in the parable comes up that evening as usual. And this time he sees a figure making its way along the road . . . a beggar, perhaps, or a laborer looking for work. Oh! He recognizes that walk! His heart tells him that it is his son. But why should we try to paraphrase the Gospel text, which is so expressive in its brevity? *But while he was yet at a distance, his father saw him and had compassion, and ran and embraced him and kissed him.*

It still looks like a dream. The world is still all upside-down. Instead of waiting gravely for the sinner to come before him, the father rushes to meet his son. Wait. Wait? He has been waiting for him far too long already! He won't wait another minute! And in spite of his age he runs like a young man toward the boy who is approaching so shamefacedly. But what about his dignity? What about the respect due to parental authority? Well, what about his love?

God's happiness

The father can't wait to hold his beloved son in his arms once more: he falls on his neck and clasps him to his breast, though his son's clothes are dirty and stink of the pigsty. He hugs him close. The son is only just able to get out the words he has prepared: *"Father, I have sinned against heaven and before you; I am no longer worthy to be called your son."* The father doesn't want to hear any more. His son doesn't even manage to finish his speech: *"Treat me as one of your hired servants,"* because his father has caught his son's beloved head between his hands and is covering it with kisses.

His son can't understand it. What is his father thinking of, to be treating him like this? Neither can we understand it at all, sage moralists that we are. Morality seems to have gone by the board. Sin is, after all, a rebellion and an offense. Can God allow the laws of his justice to be ignored?

But sin is not only an evil; it is our misfortune, our greatest misfortune. And because of that, sin, which does indeed offend God's holiness, at the same time moves him to pity: he *had compassion,* the parable says. Sin separates us from God; repentance draws God toward the sinner. This sinner who is returning is his child, who was lost and is found. He was thought to be dead, and he has come back. He's alive!

No, the son can't understand it at all. He was expecting a little place, the last place of all, in the house he had dishonored. He was counting on a morsel of bread . . . and now they are about to kill the fatted calf for him.

He had been thinking about himself. He hadn't thought about how happy he was going to make his father and the whole house. Sinners! Too concerned, by our very nature, with ourselves and our salvation! Do we recognize that when we are converted we make God and the whole Church happy? Yet this is the lesson we learn from the three parables of God's mercy: rejoicing in Heaven, the joy of the angels, the father's happiness... "more joy in heaven over one sinner who repents than over ninety-nine righteous persons who need no repentance."

The true seriousness of sin

If Jesus hadn't told us this so clearly, could we ever have imagined that before God makes us happy, we can make him happy... we have to make him happy? And that in returning to him, we fill the kingdom of Heaven with joy? We didn't know that our Father was our happiness. Besides making us see that, Jesus also gives us a glimpse of the peace and happiness of God. And it is only then, looking at it from the viewpoint Jesus has revealed to us, that we discover the seriousness of sin; not when we take the measure of our heedlessness, our falsehood, or our shame; not when we experience the painful results of our faults; but only when we try to fathom how happy it makes God when we come back to him. Only then do we finally understand the sorrow our sins have caused him. No, we didn't know that our sin was so serious. We didn't know that we had nearly left our Father in mourning for all eternity. We were depriving him of one of his children forever. He had lost us. We had killed in ourselves the life he had given us.

His happiness reveals to me the evil I have done. Why? Why the singing? Why the banquet? Why the dancing? The excessive rejoicing, the unbelievable welcome, make me see at one and the same time how happy he is and the danger I had been in: *this son of mine was dead and is alive again.*

The prodigal son finally understands where he has come back from. And grasp this point: it is only now that he is converted. He wasn't converted when he was dying of hunger; he wasn't converted when he was painfully retracing his steps home. It is in his father's arms that his conversion takes place. This is why the parable tells us no more of what the prodigal says, even though he is repentant. From the spot where father and son meet, we go straight to the courtyard of the farm and hear the father giving the servants his orders.

6. A Change of Heart

A new man

God, who ran to meet the sinner, cannot contain himself for joy . . . and he is going to turn his sinful creature into a new man.

We no longer recognize the former swineherd. Instead of his rags he is now wearing a new robe: the best the servants could find in the wardrobes, the one most skillfully woven by the women of the house. His dirty, aching feet have been washed, and he has got good new shoes on. On his finger there shines a gold ring, to mark him out as a son of the family. In his overwhelming joy, the father's one thought is to have a party. He sends some of his servants to invite guests in. Others go to fetch musicians and dancers: *manducemus et epulemur,* let us eat and celebrate!

As for the younger son, he lets them do as they like. There is nothing else he can do. If he had been asked, he would probably have preferred a more intimate meal. But his father is so happy to be telling everyone about the return of the son he had been missing!

That is the point of the parable: the son he had been missing. Like the shepherd—the lost sheep was the hundredth, but she was the one he was missing! Like the parable of the woman who drops her ten drachmas and searches for just one until she finds it. After all that, you would not want the repentant prodigal, out of a desire to punish himself, to announce that he was going to have his dinner in the kitchen with the hired servants, and refuse to sit down at his father's side at the sumptuously prepared table. How much suffering he would have caused his father, and what an insult he would have offered him! Under the pretext of his unworthiness, it would really have been his self-love that was still refusing his father's love. Then he would not really be converted. Then the whole story would have to begin again: selfishness would have triumphed once more over God's love. But he is converted. And he is going to let himself be won over by his father's love. Never again must he remind him of his former ingratitude and his unworthy behavior. He must never even speak of it! He has only to let himself be loved and never leave his father again. He must rejoice with his father to show him how certain he is of his love—he, the son who was lost and found, the child who died and has come back to life.

More than one Christian, each time they meditate on this parable, will recall their sad personal experiences, serious or less so, their errors, their faults . . . a long series of offenses that belong, thank God, to the past, now happily buried under the abundance of God's mercy. You are right: yes, thank God, and forever. The whole of the rest of your life is not long enough for you to thank our Lord sufficiently for having restored you to his friendship.

But there is another consideration we should all of us make—both those who have offended God gravely and those, probably the larger number, whom his grace has preserved from that misfortune. Are we not all miserable sinners? And don't we all have to regret the fact that we are still not fully converted? This lack of full conversion torments the most sensitive consciences. What is in reality the effect of every retreat is to be reconverted to our Lord. So, to conclude our meditation, I will remind you finally that we are not converted once and for all, and that we are not converted on our own.

A new conversion every day

First, we are not converted once and for all. One writer, who died recently, was able, without straining his imagination, to picture the prodigal son finally finding himself unable to bear it in his father's house after his return and leaving it once again, this time forever. I prefer to suppose that every day he found he had to throw himself anew into the arms of the father who had forgiven him so generously. The boy was not immune to the sort of memories that we may try to drive out but that keep returning to take hold of our minds. Still less was he immune to the sudden stirrings of passion. He needed to find afresh every morning the joy that shone in his father's eyes. Every day he needed to receive the kiss that purified him once again. We are not converted all in one go. "Don't believe," wrote Origen in the third century, "that changing your life is something you can do all at once. Every day you need to renew that newness of life."

What is conversion in fact? "The kingdom of God is at hand," says Jesus, *"be converted,"* which is often translated as *do penance*. But the Greek word that corresponds most faithfully to the equivalent expression in Hebrew is *metanoia*, the turning around of the whole person, mind, heart, and will . . . it's a true transformation, a conversion. And it is no exaggeration to say that our whole Christian life is one continual conversion.

Conversion is not, as some people imagine, a precondition for beginning a Christian life, a sort of antechamber through which one must pass to be admitted to the kingdom. It is the permanent state of the Christian life. And this radical transformation, which is aimed at making us into God's children, is never complete.

Naturally, we need to make a continuous effort to turn toward God. Naturally, we find within ourselves tendencies to self-will, self-assertion, ambition, riches, pleasure-seeking . . . all the tendencies of nature that St. Paul called "the desires of the flesh which are opposed to the desires of the spirit."

Naturally, our past faults have left traces in us, marks or folds like the folds in a piece of paper or material; the crease is set. St. Augustine was quite familiar with the hold exerted by his vanities and defects, his "former friends" as he calls them in his *Confessions*, which, he writes, came and tugged at his clothes, his flesh, whispering softly, " 'What, will you send us away? Are we never to be with you any more?' What things did they try to recall to my mind, O God! What terrible deeds! And they did not face me openly, and honestly oppose me; they would whisper behind my back, and the overmastering force of habit would say to me, 'Do you really imagine you can live without them?' "

Unquestionably, the practice of Christian life, with constant recourse to the sacraments, weakens our attraction toward evil. But it would be highly presumptuous to think that this attraction will ever disappear completely. If we thought that, we would be exposing ourselves to unexpected attacks, and we would be taken disastrously by surprise; all the more so because we live in a world of sin, which surrounds us with endless temptations to do wrong or, at the very least, invitations to mediocrity.

Daily conversion is not, thank God, a change due after a grave sin committed the day before. No. It is *daily* in the sense that every day sees the need for us to get back on our feet and reorient ourselves. The same goes for those who have advanced farther along the way of perfection, those who are not content just to fulfill their duties but who aim to refuse God nothing whatever, who are guided by love. But who can fail to recognize that love is even more totalitarian than duty? Its demands are greater, more specific, more restricting. Probably, when the accent is on love, the effort is not so hard. But that effort is more complete, more absorbing. It too requires a constant turning around.

Don't be surprised, then, that you have not yet become the perfect, finished Christians you would like to be. *Ipse perficiet*, St. Peter tells us, "God will himself perfect us," in glory. Here below we will never be *perfecti*, perfect, but *proficientes*, we will always be on the way. And Jesus told us, as we read in St. Matthew: *Estote perfecti*, "be perfect." It is an imperative, yes, but a future imperative.

This conviction shouldn't discourage us. Above all, it shouldn't lead us to slacken in our struggle. It constantly obliges us to make a new effort, day after day.

We are not converted on our own

Once we have grasped that first point, the next thing for us to understand is that we are not converted on our own.

Perhaps there are some resolutions we need to make around this point, because if our efforts at conversion have sometimes proved to be short-lived or ineffective, it is less the result of lack of willpower than of using a faulty method: we put the cart before the horse. I mean we put the human before the divine. For example, there are people who think conversion means correcting a fault, our besetting sin, by systematic, well-thought-out action; by applying control and punishments.... That sort of endeavor is a purely human undertaking which, at best, may improve our character, humanly speaking; but that is not actually being converted.

There is nothing more deceptive than the notion of making progress in one virtue. True progress is in *virtue*, that is, for Christians, in love of God, shown in obedience to all the things he wants. By attacking one fault in particular, we are setting up an artificial compartmentalization. We haven't got someone inside us who is proud, someone else who is untruthful, and someone else who is lazy.... It is one and the same person who is all that. And that is the person who needs to be converted whole and entire. Conversion is less a matter of changing our behavior than of changing ourself. Conversion is a movement of the whole person whose *result* will be the correction of our faults and the practice of the virtues.

Another example: for some people, being converted means detaching themselves from something, from a habit, a fantasy, or sometimes from a person who has a harmful effect on them. But that equally, is the result of conversion, not conversion itself. If they are not converted already, the detachment they seek is either impossible or else short-lived. Why? Because man is an incomplete being who needs completion and seeks what will complete him. You can say to someone, "Give up your money, which is having dire effects on you; give up those honors, which are bad for you; drop that friendship, that pleasure. . . ." He knows he should do all that, but if he did, then he would be left hanging, with no support at all. What he needs first of all is to find something to hold on to that is more beautiful, greater, more useful than anything else. Then he isn't just left hanging; then he isn't loveless. Then a greater attachment fills him, and he can break the ties that held him back in evil or simply in a state of imperfection.

"I renounce Satan, and I bind myself to Jesus forever."

A convert who has just received Baptism pronounces these words; but would he renounce Satan if he had not first come to know Jesus Christ? The same with us. It is not because we have renounced Satan that we attach ourselves to Jesus Christ but the other way around. The merchant in the parable did not sell all he possessed until he had found the pearl of great price. And, as we have just seen, it is because the prodigal came back to his father and let himself be hugged that he was able to become a new man. It was in his father's arms that he first understood the seriousness of his sin; it was in his father's arms that he was converted and became like a little child, a little child who could begin his life anew.

On intimate terms with Jesus Christ

Let's get it firmly into our heads that it is Jesus Christ who converts us. It is he who turns us around and changes us till we are completely transformed. Being converted does not mean first detaching ourselves from evil, from the evil that attracts us and promises us happiness—a short-lived happiness and really only a mirage, but a sort of happiness, otherwise we would not sin. But being converted means first of all turning *toward* Jesus Christ; turning toward him constantly, to find in him a greater happiness, a joy that is higher, that goes deeper than any other. That is what turns us away from evil.

A faulty method lays undue stress on the renunciation. It's true that detachment is indispensable. Our Lord has told us so quite clearly. But you must admit that to give something up just for the sake of giving it up would be absurd. It stands to reason that we can do without a lesser thing only when we possess something greater. I can say No to my pride, to money, to pleasures . . . because I have said Yes to Jesus, because I have discovered in Jesus another sort of riches, one that is still greater.

It is Jesus who turns us away from evil. If only I could understand his love for me, let myself be won over by his love . . . until I am just one thing with him. Then, not on my own but both of us together: I holding on to his hand, he pulling my arm—then I could really turn away from sin and detach myself from evil.

That is the true culmination of conversion—the conversion that is never completed, that we must always be redoing, and that lasts our whole lifetime—to become one thing with Jesus Christ. That is the last word in Christian life.

I suggest, then, as a subject for your examination of conscience, to consider what place intimacy with our Lord has in your life. Look and see if the defects you see in yourself, the times you have stood still, the times you have fallen back—which are certainly due to a slackening of your will and reluctance to make an effort—whether all these things are not initially caused by your neglect or abandonment of prayer. If you find it so difficult to detach yourself from evil, might it not be because you have detached yourself a little from our Lord?

What room do you make for prayer every day? Is it enough? Do you always keep to it? Your morning prayer! The prodigal looking into his father's eyes before taking up the day's work again. Ask yourself what your prayer is really like: is it truly a friendly conversation with our Lord? Do you take care to feed that conversation by reading the Gospel and meditating on what you read?

Perhaps you complain that you don't feel like praying? In that case it is your faith itself that is at risk. Do you really believe that our Lord loves you? Then just stop thinking about yourself altogether! Don't refuse him those few minutes of closeness, even if your heart is cold, even if your mind is blank, even if you can't think of anything to say. Our Lord knows your difficulties. It is he who is calling you, he who is waiting for you, every day. He is the one who has something to say to you. "God in his goodness," writes St. Francis de Sales, "has even greater pleasure in giving us these graces than we have in receiving them."

The power to make God happy

The prodigal never thought how happy he was going to make his father. And we too forget that God is happy when he sees us coming toward him. It's unbelievable, I grant you. We could never have known this truth if the Son of God had not come down from Heaven to tell us so. But he has told us: "My father loves you."

When you make the Sign of the Cross in the morning, when you kneel down at night, when you lift up your thoughts to him in the midst of the day's occupations, when you make a detour to go into a church and pray for a while . . . every time you do these things, you are making him happy. His child is not lost, his child is not dead, his child is still with him.

I leave you with this overwhelming truth, unbelievable as it seems: we have the power to make God happy.